SPY DOG
BRAINWASHED

ANDREW COPE

Illustrated by James de la Rue

PUFFIN

PUFFIN BOOKS

Published by the Penguin Group
Penguin Books Ltd, 80 Strand, London WC2R ORL, England
Penguin Group (USA) Inc., 375 Hudson Street, New York, New York 10014, USA
Penguin Group (Canada), 90 Eglinton Avenue East, Suite 700, Toronto, Ontario, Canada M4P 2Y3
(a division of Pearson Penguin Canada Inc.)
Penguin Ireland, 25 St Stephen's Green, Dublin 2, Ireland (a division of Penguin Books Ltd)
Penguin Group (Australia), 707 Collins Street, Melbourne, Victoria 3008, Australia
(a division of Pearson Australia Group Pty Ltd)
Penguin Books India Pvt Ltd, 11 Community Centre, Panchsheel Park, New Delhi – 110 017, India
Penguin Group (NZ), 67 Apollo Drive, Rosedale, Auckland 0632, New Zealand
(a division of Pearson New Zealand Ltd)
Penguin Books (South Africa) (Pty) Ltd, Block D, Rosebank Office Park, 181 Jan Smuts Avenue,
Parktown North, Gauteng 2193, South Africa

Penguin Books Ltd, Registered Offices: 80 Strand, London WC2R ORL, England

puffinbooks.com

First published 2013
001

Text copyright © Andrew Cope and Ann Coburn, 2013
Illustrations copyright © James de la Rue, 2013
All rights reserved

The moral right of the author and illustrator has been asserted

Set in Bembo
Typeset by Palimpsest Book Production Limited, Falkirk, Stirlingshire
Made and printed in Great Britain by Clays Ltd, St Ives plc

British Library Cataloguing in Publication Data
A CIP catalogue record for this book is available from the British Library

ISBN: 978-0-141-34427-0

www.greenpenguin.co.uk

ALWAYS LEARNING   PEARSON

Contents

1. Hunter

The rabbit sat up on its hind legs and scanned the field. It was just before sunrise, the best time for rabbits to be out, when cats and foxes had finished hunting for the night, and humans and dogs were still asleep. That morning, the field seemed as peaceful as ever but the rabbit was nervous; it could sense danger.

It peered at the row of houses on the edge of the field and then turned to gaze at the new building that stood alone on the far side, dark against the lightening sky.

Nothing stirred.

With a final flick of its ears, the rabbit settled down to nibble some juicy dandelion leaves.

Whoosh!

A shadow fell from the sky and slammed into the rabbit; its squeal was cut off as sharp claws

1

gripped its neck. When the shadow rose up again, the rabbit hung limp from its talons.

The sun rose higher, lighting up the flat roof of the new building that stood on the far side of the field. A woman stepped to the edge of the roof and stretched out her arm. She wore a leather gauntlet. The winged shadow flew to the woman, dropped the dead rabbit at her feet and landed on her wrist. It was a huge golden eagle.

'Well done, my pretty,' said the woman, holding out her other hand with a strip of raw meat gripped in her long, red-painted finger-nails.

The bird gulped down the meat and then lifted its head to stare at the woman with fierce, orange eyes. The woman stared back with eyes just as fierce and bright. Her tawny hair flicked out from her head like two wings, and her nose was hooked like a beak.

'We are both hunters, you and I,' rasped the woman. 'But I hunt for human prey.' She turned away from the bird and glared at the town spread out in front of her. Curtains were being opened in bedroom windows as people started their day. 'Soon I, Harriet Hawk, will

control them all, and they will make me the richest woman in the world!'

Harriet Hawk let out a harsh, cawing laugh and the bird on her arm spread its massive wings and screeched in reply.

2. Hunted

Lara watched Spud and Star trudge towards her. Star's sticky-up ear was drooping and Spud's tail was tucked between his legs. It looked as though their mission had not gone well. She frowned at her pups over the top of her shades. 'Give me a progress report, Spy Pups.'

'We lost our target, Ma,' Star whimpered. 'He crawled through a hole in the hedge –'

'– and escaped back into enemy territory,' finished Spud glumly.

'How do you know that?' Lara asked. 'Did you watch him go all the way through to the other side?'

'No,' woofed Star. 'We only saw him crawl *into* the hedge.' She looked at her brother. 'Ma's right. He could still be hiding in there . . .'

'Probably waiting to ambush us,' growled

Spud. His tail began to wag. 'But an ambush only works when you're not expecting it – which means we're still in the game, sis! Let's go!' he yapped, galloping to one end of the hedge.

Star's sticky-up ear sprang to attention again. 'Pincer movement!' she woofed, racing to the other end.

Lara smiled to herself as she watched her pups commando-crawl their way along the bottom of the hedge, with their noses to the ground and their bottoms in the air. For weeks they had been trying to sneak up on Marmalade, next door's new kitten, but they had never quite managed to catch him.

They won't catch him today either, Lara thought, looking at the top of the hedge. Neither of her pups had noticed that the kitten had climbed up through the middle of the hedge and was now sitting on the top, calmly cleaning his fur while they searched for him below.

Marmalade, one – Spud and Star, nil! I'll leave them to it, Lara decided, settling back into her deckchair. *Chasing Marmalade will keep them busy until Professor Cortex is ready to show them the new gadgets he's brought along.*

She looked fondly at her old friend, who was

sitting in the deckchair next to her in the Cooks' back garden. She had known Professor Cortex since she was a pup, when he had chosen her to be the world's first ever Spy Dog. 'Lara' had stood for Licensed Assault and Rescue Animal, and her code name had been GM451. A few years – and a few bullet holes – later she had retired from active duty and come to live with the Cooks, her adopted family. Now Professor Cortex was training her pups, Spud and Star. They had already qualified as Spy Dogs and were waiting for Professor Cortex to decide when they would be ready for their first proper mission.

And they're becoming very impatient, especially since New York! Lara sighed as she remembered that rather too exciting family trip, where Spud and Star had saved her and the whole Cook family from certain death *and* trapped two baddies for the FBI. *I suppose home life must seem very boring to them, after that*, thought Lara, looking around the quiet garden where every-one was gathered.

'Wonderful lunch, Mrs C,' said Professor Cortex.

'Thank you,' said Mrs Cook. 'The fresh

vegetables were from the school allotment. The children grew them.'

Ben, Sophie and Ollie all beamed with pride. They had spent long hours at the allotment after school, digging, planting, watering and fertilizing, but it had been worth it.

'Well done, children,' said Professor Cortex. 'Super veg! And Mrs C, your apple pie rules the world!'

Mrs Cook blushed. 'Oh, that old pie? That's nothing special.'

'Not true, dear,' said Mr Cook, from the goldfish pond, where he and Ben were using nets to scoop slimy green pondweed into a bucket. 'That's a very special pie. I can never resist a second slice. And it shows,' he added, patting his belly.

Same here, Lara thought, looking down at her stomach. Even her thick black and white fur could not hide a growing pooch paunch. *I may have stopped dodging bullets, but being retired has its own dangers – killer apple pies!*

'Did you two like it?' asked ten-year-old Sophie, looking up from her book to smile at Agents T and K, Professor Cortex's personal bodyguards. They were sitting next to her on the picnic blanket, balancing cups of tea on their knees and trying not to crease their smart black suits. Agent K had a slim, black leather case handcuffed to his left wrist. The case held the professor's prototype gadgets.

'Affirmative,' said Agent T.

Agent K gave a satisfied belch. 'Copy that.'

'Piepiepie-in-the-sky,' panted Ollie, bouncing higher and higher on the trampoline.

'How does he do that after a big meal without throwing up?' asked Ben, watching his little brother.

'He's six years old,' said Mr Cook, as though that explained everything.

Just then, Ollie bounced high enough to see the top of the hedge. 'Kittiekittiekittie!' he shouted, catching sight of Marmalade.

Spud and Star both stopped dead and looked at one another.

'I think we've been Marmalized,' woofed Spud.

Together, the pups stepped away from the hedge and looked upwards.

'At last!' barked Lara. 'He's been sitting up there for ages, waiting for you to notice him.'

'You could've told us, Ma,' spluttered Spud.

'Where's the fun in that?' asked Lara. 'Besides, you've just learnt a good lesson: keep your eyes peeled! A Spy Dog must always be observant.'

'Watch out!' barked Star. 'He's attacking!'

Spud looked up just as Marmalade knocked an old nest from the top of the hedge. It fell on to his head.

'Nice hat!' yapped Star.

An old shuttle-cock fell next, landing neatly over Star's sticky-up ear.

'Yours is cuter,' woofed Spud.

'Mhee-hee-hee-how!' laughed Marmalade, sticking his head over the edge again.

'That puss is making us look silly! Let's shake him down!' growled Star.

The pups both grabbed a branch of the hedge and shook it as hard as they could.

Marmalade yowled as he wobbled on his perch. He scrambled away from them along the top of the hedge. Spud and Star followed, spitting out leaves. As soon as Marmalade stopped, they shook the hedge again.

'Careful,' warned Lara.

'He's fine,' yapped Star, through a mouthful of leaves. But this time the kitten did more than wobble; he began to slip off the top of the hedge.

Lara grabbed the cushion from her deckchair and threw it to Spud and Star. 'Run, pups!' she barked as Marmalade fell. 'Break his fall!'

Spud and Star dived under the tumbling kitten, holding the cushion between them. The kitten landed feet first on the cushion with a look of feline superiority on his face.

'Phew!' gasped Spud. 'Marmalade was nearly toast!'

The kitten calmly stepped off the cushion and wandered to the gate at the bottom of the garden. He gave Spud and Star a cheeky glance over his shoulder before flicking his tail at them, slipping under the gate and heading off into the field behind the houses.

'Cool kittie!' said Ollie admiringly, gazing

after Marmalade. 'Cats always land on their feet,' he observed. 'And toast always lands butter side down. So,' thought Ollie aloud, 'what would happen if you strapped buttered toast to a cat's back and threw it out of a window?'

Professor Cortex's eyes widened. He reached for his note pad and started scribbling, only to be cut short by Mrs Cook.

'Silly idea, Ollie,' she frowned.

The professor sighed in half agreement and put his pencil down. 'Yes,' he muttered, 'quite silly. It would depend entirely on the dexterity of the feline, divided by the length of the fall. Plus you'd have to consider the thickness of the toast . . .'

'Thanks, Prof,' said Ben, rolling his eyes. 'You don't have to go into scientific detail about absolutely everything,' he explained.

The professor nodded once more and pushed his spectacles back up to the bridge of his nose. 'I appreciate that you might not share my passion for science, young Benjamin. But an enquiring mind is a very healthy thing. It enables me to come up with gadgets. And,' he said, looking over the top of his specs, 'I think you might find those very interesting indeed!'

The children swarmed round the professor. 'Have you brought some new inventions?' chirped Sophie.

'Stuff we can use at school?' beamed Ollie, tugging at the professor's jumper. 'Like invisibility ray guns and dinner-lady exterminators.'

Professor Cortex raised an eyebrow. 'Not quite, Master Oliver.' He nodded at Agent K, who unclipped the briefcase from his wrist and laid it on the table. The professor fiddled with the combination and the case clicked open. 'But my enquiring scientific mind has managed to come up with these!'

The puppies and children all gasped.

3. The Appliance of Science

'I'm not one to boast, but I think I may have come up with my best inventions so far,' said Professor Cortex proudly as they all gathered round him. 'And I've got one for each of the Spy Pups.'

Star and Spud couldn't help doing a whole body wag. Lara tried to hide her disappointment but the scientist noticed a slight sag of her shoulders.

'Plus,' he beamed, 'even *retired* Spy Dogs need to have the latest technology.' Three tails wagged as the scientist reached into the case. 'Check this out, my little canine agents. A gadget you wear round your neck. I call it a "tie".'

Lara raised her eyebrows at her old boss. *I hate to break it to you, Prof, but a tie isn't exactly a new invention.*

'I'm not wearing a silly tie,' huffed Star, smoothing her fur with a paw. 'A girl likes to look good while she's spying!'

'I can see you're not impressed, but trust me,' said the professor, pulling a slim, curved device from his case.

Spud wagged enthusiastically, lifted his chin and allowed Professor Cortex to clip the device to his collar. It fitted like a second collar rather than hanging down like a tie.

'Good,' said the professor. 'Now all you need to do is press your chin down to activate the tie.'

Spud did as he was told. There was a hiss as two telescopic stalks shot out of the device and rose up on each side of his nose. When the stalks reached his eyes, a dark lens opened out from the top of each and clamped into place.

'Whoa! What's happening?! Oh . . .' Spud stopped moving. His mouth dropped open.

Lara leapt to her feet. 'Spud! Talk to me!'

'I'm fine, Ma, but everyone's turned rainbow-coloured!'

Star was wishing she'd shown more interest. 'T.I.E. stands for Thermal- imaging Eyepiece,'

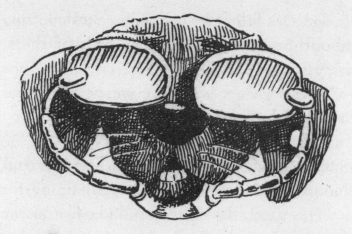

explained Professor Cortex. Agent Spud is now seeing us in a very different way.'

'Are they like night-vision goggles?' asked Sophie.

'Good guess, Sophie,' said Professor Cortex. 'But dogs already have pretty good night vision – nearly as good as cats.'

Watch it, Prof! Spud growled. He was still smarting from Ollie's 'cool kittie' comment.

'These thermal-imaging eyepieces are even better than night-vision goggles,' explained Professor Cortex. 'Spud can now see in complete darkness, but he can also see hidden people or animals in daylight. Have a look at the garden hedge, Agent Spud.'

'Wow!' gasped the puppy as he gazed at the

hedge. 'It's full of little orange specks, flitting about. Sparrows! There are loads of them, hiding inside the hedge. We could've done with this gadget when we were looking for Marmalade.'

'Thermal means heat, right?' said Ben. 'So Spud can "see" us now, because we're warm-blooded and hotter than our surroundings?'

'That's exactly right, Ben. The hotter the temperature, the hotter the colour. Red is warmest, blue is coldest.'

'The Prof's brain must be overheating,' yapped Spud. 'His bald bonce is red hot! And Agents K and T have been sitting on the grass too long. They both have blue bums. They look like a pair of baboons!'

Lara gave Professor Cortex an admiring nod. *You've surpassed yourself, Prof. I can't wait to see what retired Spy Dogs get!*

'If you liked that, Lara,' beamed Professor Cortex. 'Wait till you see the next gadget!'

Spud pressed his chin against his collar again and the TIE folded away. Star stepped eagerly forward as Professor Cortex reached into his case and brought out a tiny cylinder. 'The world's smallest torch,' he announced, glancing over the top of his spectacles. 'Small enough to be clipped on to a dog collar. But that's not why it's special.'

Tell us about the science, Prof, wagged Star.

'It's the opposite of a normal torch,' explained the professor, struggling to find the tiny switch. 'A sort of "un-torch", I suppose. Normal torches light up the dark, right?'

Children and canines nodded. Star's tongue hung out in concentration.

'Well, this one creates dark in the light.'

Star's tongue hung longer and her doggie brow furrowed as she tried to understand the professor's logic.

'Found it,' said the scientist finally, clicking the switch and turning the torch on. It was a lovely sunny day and the professor beamed the torch at the wall. A dark patch appeared, the torch casting a black shadow. 'Creates darkness. See?'

He turned the torch on Sophie, beaming it in her face.

'Yikes!' she yelled. 'Who switched off the lights?'

'Not sure of its use yet,' admitted the professor, clipping the torch on to Star's collar. 'But

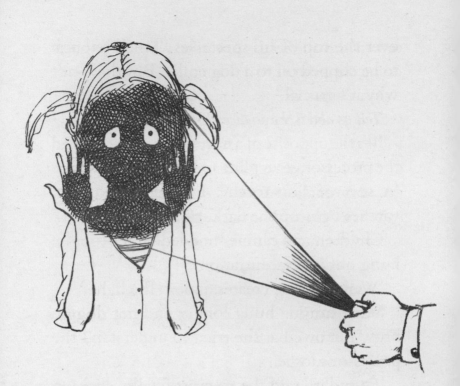

I'm sure a use will become clear ... or dark ...
whatever ... eventually.' Star was delighted,
beaming her un-torch in her brother's face.

And for newly retired canine agents? thought
Lara. *I don't want to miss out!*

The professor reached into his case and
brought out a small rubber ball. 'A marble?'
guessed Sophie.

Lara stretched her neck, allowing Professor
Cortex to fix the device to her collar. 'As you
know,' said Professor Cortex. 'I have just

returned from South America, where I've been doing some work with llamas.'

'But what use are llamas, apart from their wool?' asked Sophie. 'Spy llamas? I don't think so.'

'Actually, we're thinking of using them as guard animals,' said Professor Cortex. 'They spit, you know. It comes up from their stomachs.' He shuddered. 'Disgusting, smelly stuff. You'd have to be pretty determined to force your way through a herd of spitting llamas.'

'You should try the lunch queue at my school,' muttered Ben.

'Anyway,' continued Professor Cortex. 'I discovered that if you mix llama spit with one of my secret formulas, you get an incredibly slippery substance.'

'Like banana skins?' beamed Ollie.

'Banana skins times a thousand,' nodded the professor. 'I've invented the most slippery substance known to mankind. And I've filled those little rubber balls with it. So, if a baddie attacks, you launch a ball and they're immediately off balance.'

The professor looked round at the puzzled faces. 'Here,' he said, taking a spare ball from

his coat pocket. 'It works on grass, concrete . . .
any surface.' The scientist lobbed the ball along
the garden path and there was a small puff of
yellow smoke as it exploded.

'Look out!' shouted Mrs Cook as the garden
gate swung open, but it was too late; two beefy
men had already stepped through, right into
the path of the yellow smoke.

4. Fishy Business

The first man was short but very, very wide with massive shoulders. The second man was a big-boned giant with a cauliflower face that matched his enormous bashed-up ears. Lara winced. Either of these muscle men would hit the ground very hard indeed if they skidded on the llama spit.

Professor Cortex winced because he knew what was coming. The first man stepped forward and promptly toppled over like a skittle, making an enormous splash as he landed in the goldfish pond. The second was a step behind – he skidded over and belly-flopped right next to his friend.

Everyone jumped back from the wall of water that came hurtling their way.

'Help me, Squat!' bellowed the big-eared

giant. 'I can't swim,' he yelled, splashing his arms and gulping slimy water.

'Shut up, Dumbbell! It's a pond, you idiot,' spluttered Squat. 'It's not deep!'

Dumbbell heaved himself up before skidding on slimy weed at the bottom of the pond, his feet coming up from under him, and he landed back on Squat.

'GEROFF ME, YOU GREAT LUMP!' Squat roared.

Dumbbell hauled himself from the pond, dripping slime. Squat breaststroked his way to the side of the pool and glared at the family.

Everyone had been frozen to the spot, but now they sprang into action. Mrs Cook ran inside to get some towels and the professor and Mr Cook hurried across to help Dumbbell and Squat. Ben looked at Sophie and stifled a snigger.

Ollie laughed out loud. 'Llama spit,' he said, pointing at the men. 'Like a thousand banana skins.'

The men looked a little confused. Dumbbell sniffed a strand of pondweed up his left nostril and pulled one of Dad's koi carp from his shirt.

Spud looked at Dumbbell's green face and

big muscles. 'It's The Hulk. Don't make him angry,' he joked. 'You won't like him when he's angry.'

'Forget about Dumbbell, pups,' barked Lara. 'It's the other one who looks angry!'

'So sorry about that,' said Mr Cook, holding out his hand to a furious Squat. 'My wife's gone to fetch you a towel.'

Ignoring Mr Cook's hand, Squat lumbered to his feet and squelched across the garden. He was built like a very short tank. His neck was as thick as his head and Lara figured he was probably as wide as he was tall. Lara raised her hackles, just in case.

Mr Cook gulped and took a step back. 'Now, gentlemen, is there something I can help you with?'

'Dumbbell!' roared Squat, making the giant behind him jump. 'Leaflets!'

Dumbbell pulled some slime-smeared pieces of paper from the canvas bag at his side and handed them out.

'Hawk's Gym,' said Squat, nodding at the leaflet. 'Grand opening tonight. Harriet Hawk invites you to –'

'Did you say Harriet Hawk?' interrupted

Professor Cortex. 'I've heard about her. That woman is well on her way to taking over the world!'

Dumbbell gasped. 'How did you know tha— OWW!' He bent to clutch the foot Squat had just stamped on.

'Taking over the world? What do you mean?' demanded Squat.

'Only that Harriet Hawk has opened gyms all over the country in the last year or so,' said Professor Cortex.

'Oh. You mean *that* kind of taking over the world. That's all right then.' Squat cleared his throat and continued his sales pitch. 'Hawk's Gym. Grand opening tonight. Harriet Hawk invites you to join up and get fit fast!'

'We'll certainly join,' said Mrs Cook, hurrying up and handing Squat and Dumbbell a towel each. 'It's the least we can do after you both got soaked. What do you think, dear?'

Mr Cook hesitated.

'We could get rid of that spare tyre of yours

in no time,' said Squat, poking Mr Cook in the belly a bit too hard.

'Are you two personal trainers then?' asked Mrs Cook.

'No,' said Dumbbell. 'We're – oof!'

Lara frowned. What had Dumbbell been about to say this time? And why had Squat elbowed him in the belly to shut him up?

'Are you OK, Mr Dumbbell?' asked Sophie, looking up at the big-eared giant.

'Course he is,' said Squat, patting Dumbbell's six-pack. 'Belly like a board. We personal trainers have to be tough. Don't we, Dumbbell?'

'Yes, Squat,' the giant agreed meekly.

'What do you say, dear?' asked Mrs Cook. 'Shall we join Hawk's Gym? It's just across the field there, next to the school. Practically on our doorstep.'

'All right,' said Mr Cook reluctantly. 'We'll join.'

'See you tonight then,' said Squat, herding Dumbbell towards the gate. 'And I'll make sure you get some *very* personal training.'

'Can I come too?' called Ollie.

'No kids,' said Squat, giving Ollie one last glare over his shoulder before letting the gate slam behind him. 'Parents only,' he shouted over his shoulder as he and his mate dripped down the street in search of new recruits.

'They weren't very nice,' said Ben.

'No,' said Mr Cook, rubbing his belly where Squat had poked him too hard. 'But, like he said, personal trainers have to be tough.'

Not that tough, thought Lara. *There's something odd about those two knuckleheads. I smell fishy business – and it's not just our pond!* She peered at the leaflet Ollie had dropped. *Children might not be allowed, but it doesn't say anything about dogs. Time for me to 'get fit fast' and have a good snoop around Hawk's Gym while I'm at it!*

5. Brainwashed!

The press photographer crouched in front of Lara's treadmill and focused his camera. 'Cheese!'

Are you offering? Don't mind if I do. Lara's mouth watered at the thought of a thick slice of cheddar on a digestive biscuit. She tried not to dribble as she pounded the running treadmill; flying drool was not a good look for a photograph.

'Could you lean a bit closer to the treadmill, Mrs Hawk?' asked the photographer.

From the corner of her eye, Lara saw a face with a hooked, beak-like nose loom up beside her.

'Is that better?' asked Harriet Hawk, cracking a smile that showed all her teeth.

Lara shuddered. Harriet Hawk had given her exactly the same smile earlier that evening

when she had arrived at the gym with Mr and Mrs Cook.

'Of course Lara can join the gym,' she had said. 'The more the merrier. I've heard that your dog has had some adventures,' she cackled. 'And she's a local celebrity. Lara has already been in the papers. Oh, how I love publicity.'

Once they had filled out their enrolment forms, Mr and Mrs Cook had tried out all the gym equipment while Lara had spent the evening doing as much snooping as she could. She had found nothing out of the ordinary except for the door to the basement, which was made of reinforced steel and had a code-operated lock. She had been about to investigate further, when Harriet Hawk had collared her and pushed her on to a running treadmill as a publicity stunt for the newspaper photographer.

Lara could see the door now, on the far wall, behind the photographer's head. *Nobody installs that kind of security just to protect a bit of cleaning equipment and a pool filter pump. What's really behind that door, I wonder?*

'Can we get your, er, handsome assistants in the picture too?' asked the photographer.

'Of course,' said Harriet Hawk, waving Squat and Dumbbell over to join her.

'Perfect,' said the photographer. 'Hold still now.'

Wish I could, Lara thought, pounding the treadmill and trying to suck in her tummy at the same time as the camera flashed. *But if I don't keep moving I'll fly off the back of this thing!*

'All finished, thanks, Mrs Hawk,' said the photographer. 'It'll be in the local paper tomorrow.'

'And on global news the day after,' she muttered, smiling under her breath. As soon as the photographer turned away, Harriet Hawk switched off her smile and reached for the controls on Lara's treadmill.

At last! I really need a breather, Lara panted.

But Harriet Hawk's long red nails did not press the Off button; instead they tapped the arrow that increased the treadmill speed. 'No pain, no gain, mutt!' she hissed, and let out a shrill, cawing laugh.

Lara picked up her pace, her chest beginning to heave.

Squat leant closer to his boss. 'Have you picked your targets yet, Mrs Hawk?' he asked, out of the corner of his mouth.

Targets? Lara's ears pricked up as she pounded the treadmill.

Harriet Hawk nodded and held up the gym-membership forms everyone had filled in. 'There are twenty here who qualify. I'll go and talk to them while you and Dumbbell get rid of the ones we don't want.'

'Including this mutt?' asked Squat, jerking his head at Lara.

'No, she'll have to stay because I want her owners to stay,' said Harriet Hawk. 'They qualify as targets.'

Mr and Mrs Cook are targets? For what? Lara was so shocked she stopped running, but the treadmill belt kept moving. Her paws flew out from under her and she shot off the back of the treadmill with her bottom in the air.

Ouch! Carpet burn, she winced as she skidded across the floor on her nose before slamming into a wall with a loud thud. When other gym users looked round to see what the noise was, Lara sprang up with a flourish and did a few stretches. *I'm fine! Nothing to look at here!*

Mrs Cook sprinted across to her. 'Are you all right, Lara?'

'Don't worry, Mrs Cook, no bones broken,' said Harriet Hawk. 'We'll keep an eye on your pooch. You carry on with your exercise.'

'I think my husband's had enough for one night,' said Mrs Cook as a red-faced Mr Cook staggered towards them on rubbery legs. 'Haven't you, dear?'

Mr Cook could only nod and wheeze, clutching his side.

Good decision! Lara headed for the exit with a sigh of relief, but Harriet Hawk stepped in front of her, blocking the way.

'Oh, that's a shame, Mrs Cook. I was hoping

the two of you might join my Ultra-Gym Squad. The pooch can stay too, of course. She could lose a little weight around the middle.'

Cheek! Lara glared at Harriet Hawk. *I'm big-boned!*

'Did you say Ultra-Gym?' Mr Cook straightened up and stuck out his chest. 'That sounds exclusive.'

'Very,' said Harriet Hawk. 'Invitation only. A hand-picked special class after the gym has closed. A guaranteed six-pack.' She looked around as if trying to keep the next sentence secret. 'And it's free.'

'Did you hear that, dear?' said Mr Cook, looking pleased and proud. 'We've been hand-picked.'

'That's nice, but we told Ollie we'd be back before his bedtime. We should go.'

Lara nodded furiously in agreement, but stopped when she noticed Squat looking at her oddly.

'Ollie won't mind,' said Mr Cook. 'Not when he's got Mrs Brown from next door looking after him and spoiling him rotten. A six-pack tummy. And it's free, dear,' he reminded her.

'Well . . . all right. Just this once,' said Mrs Cook.

'Once is all I need,' murmured Harriet Hawk, so quietly that only Lara heard her.

A few minutes later, Squat and Dumbbell had cleared the gym of everyone except Harriet Hawk's chosen twenty. They were all lined up on the row of treadmills, in front of the big screens on the gym wall. Lara had taken the end treadmill because it was close to the reinforced steel basement door. Mr and Mrs Cook were next to her. As she marched on her treadmill, Lara glanced along the row, trying to spot what made all these people into suitable targets, but they seemed to have nothing in common as far as she could see – just twenty adults of different shapes and sizes.

'Watch the screens, everyone,' called Harriet Hawk. 'In a minute they'll show you what to do.' She nodded to Squat and he hurried across to the steel door and punched a security code into the keypad. Lara leant over so far trying to see that she nearly flew off the back of the treadmill a second time, but Squat was blocking the keypad with his body.

Drat! As Lara scrabbled back into the middle

of her treadmill, Squat opened the door to the basement, revealing the first few steps of a metal staircase. He clattered down the steps and, a minute later, the screens stopped showing the latest music video. Instead, Harriet Hawk's face appeared. Her strange bright eyes seemed to pulse and glow. Lara waited for their exercise instructions, but Harriet Hawk just kept on staring out of the screens. 'Look into my eyes,' she soothed. 'And relax . . .'

Twenty sets of feet pounded the treadmills, all eyes glued to Harriet Hawk's pulsing pupils.

Huh! The DVD must be stuck. Lara glanced sideways at Mr and Mrs Cook. They were marching in step, gazing open-mouthed at the screens as though the eyes of Harriet Hawk were the most fascinating things they had ever seen. Lara looked up at the screen. Harriet Hawk's unblinking eyes had gone orange and her pupils were pulsating. Lara forced herself to look away. *What's going on?* Lara looked past Mr and Mrs Cook along the line of treadmills. Every single person was staring adoringly at the screens as they marched. Their eyes were wide and unblinking. Then, as though they had all been given a signal, they snapped their arms across their chests, fists clenched in a salute.

'WE WILL OBEY HARRIET HAWK,' they chanted in unison. 'WE WILL OBEY!'

Lara gulped. *They're acting like zombies!*

Harriet Hawk, Squat and Dumbbell were moving along the line of treadmills now, staring into each face. Dumbbell clapped his hands centimetres from the nose of a tall fair-haired man, Squat slapped an overweight man's belly and Harriet Hawk scratched her long red nails down the arm of a friendly-looking dark-haired woman. They all just kept marching.

'It worked,' said Harriet Hawk. 'We've got them! They're all brainwashed.'

'What about the mutt? Has it worked on her?' asked Squat.

Yikes, thought Lara. *Time for some quick thinking and Oscar-winning acting.* All three of them walked across to Lara's treadmill. She stared straight ahead and tried to look as vacant as she could. Dumbbell leant down and blew into her face. *Phew! Dog-breath!* Squat went behind the treadmill and gave her tail a yank. Lara just managed to stop herself yelping with shock. *I'll get you back for that*, she vowed silently.

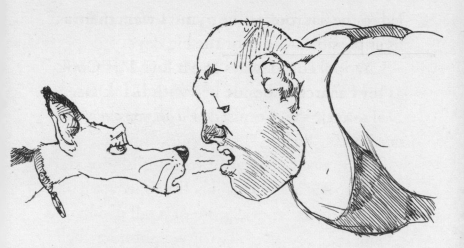

Finally, Harriet Hawk hooked one of her sharp red nails through the bullet-hole in Lara's sticky-up ear and twisted it back and forth. Tears of pain sprang to Lara's eyes but she made herself keep on marching as though nothing was happening.

'Well, well, well,' said Harriet Hawk, letting go of Lara's ear. 'The brainwashing works on dogs too!'

No, it doesn't, you evil bird-faced lady, thought Lara. *I always knew doggie brainwaves were superior. Now I have proof!*

'Good. The final squad in my zombie army is now in place. Keep them marching,' ordered Harriet Hawk as she headed for the stairs that led to the flat roof of the gym. 'I want them as fit as possible, ready for the big day.'

Lara looked sideways at Mr and Mrs Cook as they marched beside her with blank faces. *Don't worry*, she promised. *I'll get you out of this somehow!*

6. Eagle-eyed

'That's the little one off into dreamland,' said Mrs Brown, the Cooks' next-door neighbour, coming down the stairs from Ollie's bedroom. 'Fast asleep. What a little sweetie-pie!'

Ben, Sophie, Spud and Star were all in the kitchen. They looked at one another.

'*Sweetie-pie?*' whispered Sophie.

Ben stuck two fingers in his mouth and pretended to be sick.

'Custard pie, more like!' yapped Spud. 'And Ollie would be the one throwing it!'

'That's more his style,' agreed Star, looking at the red splodge on the ceiling where Ollie had rocket-fired his tomato ketchup at teatime.

'Speaking of pie,' said Mrs Brown as she bustled into the kitchen and filled the kettle, 'how about a cup of tea and some of my home-made chocolate tart?'

'Yes, please!' said Ben and Sophie, from the kitchen table where they were doing their homework.

'Yes, please!' woofed Spud and Star.

Spud's tail began to wag as he watched Mrs Brown lift a cake tin from her bag. He loved it when their next-door neighbour came to babysit; she was the best baker in the village. *A slice of her chocolate tart might just make up for putting up with that pesky new kitten all evening*, he thought, giving Marmalade a glare. The kitten was sitting on the bench next to the kitchen sink. He narrowed his eyes at Spud and then, with a flick of his paw, splashed him with cold washing-up water.

'Watch it!' yapped Spud, leaping to his feet.

Marmalade scooted over to Mrs Brown, pretending to be scared.

'Oh dear, did the naughty doggywoggy fwiten my ickle Marmaladywady?' said Mrs Brown, frowning at Spud. 'Behave now, Spud, or no chocolate tart for you!'

The ultimate punishment! Spud took a deep breath to calm down, but then Marmalade peeked over Mrs Brown's shoulder and stuck out a pink tongue at him.

'Come down here and do that!' barked Spud.

'Chill out, bro,' woofed Star, jumping down from the kitchen table where she had been helping Sophie with her maths. 'Marmalade wants you to lose your cool. He would just love it if you missed out on the chocolate tart!'

Spud groaned and sat down again. Marmalade jumped from the bench to the floor and

stalked past him to the back door, but Spud
hardly noticed. He was watching Mrs Brown
cut the chocolate tart into thick slices. *Slurp!*
His mouth was watering.

'Miaow!' cried the kitten. 'Mmiiaaooww!'

'Oh, does my ickleMarmaladywady want
to peepee?' crooned Mrs Brown, abandoning
the chocolate tart and rushing to open the
door.

'Good riddance!' yapped Spud as the kitten
stepped out into the garden.

'You too, Spud?' said Mrs Brown. 'Out you
go then.'

'No, I wasn't barking to go out, thanks. I'll
stay for the tart,' slurped Spud, but Mrs Brown
hooked her foot under his bum and shoved him
out of the house. Star was pushed out next and
the back door was closed before they could get
back into the kitchen.

The pups stood in the back garden, their eyes
becoming accustomed to the dark. Marmalade
sniggered as he slipped under the back gate and
into the field.

'He did that on purpose!' yapped Star. 'Time
to marmalize Marmalade! Ready, bro?'

Spud pressed his chin down on to his collar

to activate the TIE. 'Ready,' he woofed as the thermal-imaging lenses slotted into place over his eyes. 'This is so cool!' he yapped. 'For the first time, I can see in the dark better than Marmalade. This ought to be easy!'

Spud squeezed under the gate. He got stuck halfway and his sister gave his bottom a shove. *Hmm. Maybe it's just as well I didn't have that slice of pie*, he thought as he sucked in his tum and scrabbled through to the field. The two pups set off, Spud's night-vision goggles brightening the darkness. Ahead of them, he could see a red and orange blob, with yellow legs and a green tail with a blue tip. It was Marmalade. He was halfway across the field, chasing a tiny yellow spark, which Spud guessed was a moth. *Ha! You think you're the hunter, kitty? You're not. You're the hunted!*

Spud and Star did not know it, but they were not the only ones hunting Marmalade. They had nearly reached their target when some-thing fell from the sky in front of them. The TIE goggles showed it as a huge blob of orange and red. Marmalade let out a cry of fear and pain as the blob sank its talons into his back and lifted him into the air.

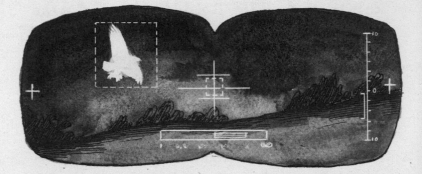

It had all happened so fast that Spud and Star were still frozen to the spot as the massive bird flew off across the field with Marmalade.

7. Hide-and-seek

'Quick!' yapped Spud, setting off after Marmalade. 'We have to rescue him!'

Star pulled herself together and sprinted after her brother. The bird was flying low over the field. 'It's looking for somewhere to land,' Spud panted, running as fast as his short legs would go.

'So it can start eating Marmalade!' sobbed Star.

'Keep chasing it, Star! If we don't let it land, it might give up and drop him!'

They raced after the bird, following its every twist and turn and yapping as loudly as they could whenever it tried to land. As he ran, Spud studied the bird through his thermal-imaging eyepieces. He clicked the magnify button for a close-up. It showed up as a brilliant splash of colour. The wings were spread across the sky like orange fans of fire. *It's an eagle*, he thought, remembering his bird identification lessons. *But eagles don't live here – what is it doing in our village?*

His legs pumped but his heart sank. How could he and Star rescue Marmalade from such a fierce and ruthless hunter? They were tiring fast and Spud and Star both knew that soon the bird would leave them behind. It swerved again but, this time, it headed straight for them.

'Duck,' yelled Spud, flinging himself to the ground.

'It's too big for a duck,' yapped Star. 'Looks like an eagle!' she barked, jumping up at the bird in a last desperate attempt to rescue Marmalade before her energy ran out. The eagle screeched and flapped its wings as it made a sharp turn to avoid colliding with the leaping puppy.

'Nooo!' yelped Spud as the huge bird began to climb into the sky. He flung out his front paws and just snagged the tip of one of the eagle's tail feathers. Startled, the bird opened its talons and let go of Marmalade.

Spud flopped on to the grass beside the limp body of the kitten and lay there, gasping for breath.

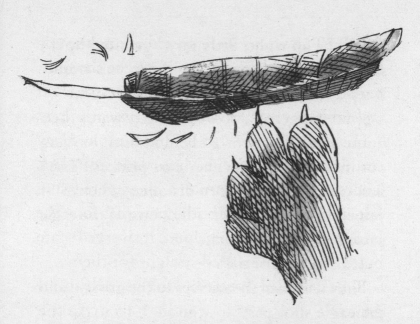

'Is he still alive?' whimpered Star, creeping closer.

Spud lifted his head and gazed at Marmalade. He saw the little chest rise and fall. 'Yes!' he gasped, scrambling to his feet. 'He's breathing!'

'Let's get him home before that horrible bird comes back,' whimpered Star, scanning the sky.

'Sling him over my back,' yapped Spud, crouching down next to Marmalade. The kitten was bleeding from cuts on his back made by the bird's sharp talons. As Star grabbed him by the scruff of the neck and pulled him on to Spud's back, Marmalade miaowed with pain.

'It'll be all right, little guy,' grunted Spud, struggling to his feet. 'We'll get you home. Keep a look out for that bird of prey, Star!'

Spud staggered across the field towards their house while Star trotted behind him, looking out into the dark sky, her ears pricked. They had only gone a short distance when Star yelped with fright as the silhouette of the eagle passed across the moon.

'It's coming for us!'

They flattened themselves to the ground and the eagle shot past, low enough to make the grass bend in the breeze.

'I think it can see the white patches on my fur,' whimpered Star. 'I wish I was black all over like you, Spud!'

'Don't be silly, sis,' said Spud, staggering to his feet and struggling onwards. 'You're always saying black and white is much more fashionable.'

'Look out!' yelped Star.

Spud dived behind a tussock of grass as the eagle whizzed past. 'This is the worst game of hide-and-seek I've ever played,' he grumbled, standing up and tottering towards the house again with Marmalade slung across his back.

A high-pitched whistle cut across the field. The pups turned to see where it had come from. Spud put his eyes back to the night-vision goggles. He spotted the outline of a woman on the flat roof of Hawk's Gym at the far side of the field. She had a hooked, beak-like nose and hair that spread out from each side of her head like a pair of wings. The woman lifted her left hand to her mouth and the whistle sounded again. Her right arm was outstretched.

'Over there,' breathed Spud, jabbing a paw

in the direction of the gym. 'Someone's calling the eagle!'

Spud commentated as the massive bird flew to the woman and landed on her outstretched arm. 'The eagle has landed,' he gasped.

Then the woman turned from the edge of the roof and walked away, carrying the giant bird with her. Spud and Star heard her shout orders down from the roof. 'Dumbbell! Squat!'

'Uh-oh,' woofed Star. 'I think that must be Harriet Hawk – the boss that those two pond-life personal trainers mentioned – and it sounds like she's calling for reinforcements!'

'Let's get out of here, quick!' yapped Spud.

8. Star Turn

'Dumbbell! Squat!' Harriet Hawk shrieked again, hurrying down the stairs from the flat roof and into the gym.

Lara blinked and nearly missed her step on the treadmill, not quite believing the size of the huge bird of prey perched on the gym owner's arm.

Dumbbell and Squat were sitting by the open basement door, playing cards and ignoring Lara and the twenty zombie exercisers as they all marched in place.

'Yes, boss?' said Squat, leaping to his feet and scattering cards everywhere. Dumbbell dropped to his knees and began to scrabble them together.

'Leave that!' snapped Harriet Hawk.

Dumbbell jumped up so fast, his enormous ears flapped like kites in the wind.

'There are two pesky pups out on the field,' Harriet Hawk continued. 'I couldn't see them, but I could hear them yapping. They frightened my poor Hercules, didn't they, my pet?' she cooed, stroking the bird's ruffled feathers.

'It's probably the same two troublemakers Dumbbell and I met earlier today,' said Squat. 'That's their mum,' he added, turning to glare at Lara.

Good for you, Spud and Star! Lara lifted her head proudly and marched with an extra spring in her step. *Spy Dogs rule!*

'I'll keep an eye on this lot,' snarled Harriet Hawk. 'You go and catch those pups. Bring them to me. We'll give them to Hercules to play with!'

Lara wanted to jump from the treadmill and run after Dumbbell and Squat, but Harriet Hawk was watching her. *I must keep pretending to be brainwashed*, she told herself. *If Spud and Star can get the better of an eagle, they'll have no trouble with those two idiots. Mr and Mrs Cook need me more, right now.* She made her eyes go blank and let a little bit of drool escape from the side of her mouth. *I will obey. I will obey. Blah blahblah*, she thought.

Satisfied, Harriet Hawk turned away and

settled Hercules on the handlebars of an exercise bike, putting a leather hood over his head to keep him calm.

Lara risked a glance at the gym door. *Stay safe, pups!*

'Here they come,' panted Spud. 'Dumb and dumber.'

'And they've got torches,' yapped Star.

'Don't worry, Star. I'm wearing my TIE. It's much better than a torch.'

'I'm not worried,' woofed Star, watching the wavering torch beams. 'We're a team, bro. You get Marmalade home. I'll keep them off your back.'

Spud nodded tiredly and staggered onwards. Star could see that carrying the unconscious kitten was wearing him out. She turned and ran towards the torches. *Spud's right*, she thought. *Black and white fur is so much better than plain black. Who'd want to fade into the crowd when you can really stand out!*

Star leapt into Dumbbell's torch beam and used it like a spotlight, in which to do a cheeky tap dance. *Ta da!*

'Here's one of them!' cried Dumbbell. 'And

it's doing a . . . dance,' he yelled, his voice trailing away in disbelief.

Star shot off to the left, out of the torch beam. Dumbbell stumbled after her, but the pup changed direction and crept round behind him and into Squat's torch beam.

'Over here, Dumbo,' she yapped. 'In the long grass.'

The men's heavy footsteps stumbled after the Spy Pup. Star was enjoying herself. She knew there was a pond up ahead and her aim was to lure the baddies to a soggy end.

'Come back, Dumbbell – this way!' yelled Squat, running towards Star.

Again, she disappeared into the darkness and popped up a minute later in Dumbbell's torch beam. With a growl, both men stumbled off after her, but Star hid in a rabbit warren and as the men stumbled by in the opposite direction, she gave a satisfied nod.

Show's over. Time to head for home.

By the time she trotted up to the Cooks' back-garden gate, Squat and Dumbbell had reached the furthest corner of the field. Star cocked her head, listening, until she heard a splash and a roar of anger.

'Great finale!' she yapped. 'That's two ponds in one day. These guys need to be more careful!'

'Well done, Star,' croaked Spud, staggering up to the gate and collapsing on to the grass. 'Brilliant performance.'

Spud slid Marmalade from his back and together they pushed the limp kitten under the gate. Once they had squeezed through after him, Spud folded his TIE away. The pups worked as a team, one on each side of the wounded kitten. They nosed their heads under his forelegs and dragged him to the kitchen door.

Spud collapsed on to the back step beside Marmalade while Star yapped and scratched to be let in. When Mrs Brown opened the door, Spud stood up, even though his legs were trembling with exhaustion.

Now I really deserve that slice of chocolate tart, he thought proudly.

But Mrs Brown was staring at him in horror as she scooped up her wounded kitten.

'What have you done to my Marmalade?' she cried. 'You bad, bad dog!'

9. Zombie Army

Lara gave a sigh of relief when Squat and Dumbbell squelched back into the gym empty-handed. *Victory to Spud and Star!*

'We lost them!' yelled Dumbbell, scooping mud out of his enormous ears.

'Stop shouting,' growled Harriet Hawk.

'Pardon?' shouted Dumbbell.

'Your ears are full of mud!' yelled Harriet Hawk.

Dumbbell shook his head, sending mud flying everywhere. 'I can't hear you! My ears are full of mud!'

Squat elbowed Dumbbell in the ribs to shut him up. 'Do you want us to keep looking for the pups, boss?'

'Forget it. Hercules can wait a little longer for his new toys,' said Harriet Hawk. 'Let's concentrate on this lot.' She studied the row of marchers. 'Good. They're fully brainwashed now. Time to get the implants ready. Come with me down to the command centre.'

As soon as the three of them had disappeared through the steel door to the basement, Lara let herself slide off the back of the treadmill. She tiptoed through the open command-centre door and out on to the top of the metal staircase. Spread out below her was a spotless white room full of electronic equipment and monitor screens. Lara noticed that the electrical flexes powering the equipment were not plugged into wall sockets. Instead they went up through the ceiling and into the gym.

Very clever, she thought. *This command centre is off-grid! All the*

power is generated by the gym users as they pedal the bikes and row on the rowing machines. It's completely self-sufficient and undetectable. What is Harriet Hawk up to that needs to be kept so secret?

Lara ducked under the handrail and leant out over the edge of the stairs. Directly below her, Dumbbell and Squat were lining up a row of twenty-one syringes on a steel tray. Lara gulped. *Oh dear! I think one of those injections might be for me – and I hate needles!*

She spotted a map of the UK, spread out on a large table. Model buildings and squads of plastic soldiers dotted the map and there were long-handled wooden rakes to move the squads around. *It's like a war room! She's planning an invasion. She's building an army!*

Lara leant out a bit further and spotted a bank of TV screens. Each one showed the inside of a different Hawk's Gym, and, in each gym, a squad of brainwashed people marched, cycled or rowed together in eerie silence. *Except this is going to be a zombie army!*

Lara felt her hackles rise. *It's my duty as a Spy Dog to find out what her evil plan is – and it's my duty as a family mutt to save Mr and Mrs Cook while I'm at it!*

'Seventy-nine Zombie squads!' squealed Harriet Hawk, clapping with glee. 'All brainwashed and ready to obey. Soon,' she said, standing tall and looking down her nose, 'I'll be the wealthiest, most powerful woman in the world.'

'And us, boss?' said Squat, nearly dropping the tray of syringes in excitement. 'We'll be rich too?'

'I suppose so,' sighed Harriet Hawk.

'And powerful?' gasped Dumbbell.

The boss rolled her eyes, trying her best to imagine a pair of rich and powerful idiots. 'And powerful,' she droned. 'But you'll be neither, unless we get the new recruits injected and move our ingenious plan to the next level.'

Harriet Hawk pressed a button and the dark screen in the centre of the display lit up. 'Squad number eighty,' she announced. The screen showed Mr and Mrs Cook and the other new recruits marching in place. At the end of the row of machines, there was an empty treadmill where Lara was supposed to be.

Lara groaned under her breath. *Oops!*

For one long second, nobody moved. Then

Harriet Hawk, Dumbbell and Squat all swivelled their heads and looked up to the top of the stairs, straight at Lara.

10. Oscar

Lara nearly turned and ran, but then she had a better idea. She began to march in place at the top of the stairs, banging her head against the handrail with every step she took.

'Squat! Bring the syringes,' ordered Harriet Hawk as she headed up the stairs.

Lara kept marching, staring straight ahead and nutting the handrail. *This had better work*, she thought. *I'm getting a very sore bonce!*

'I see what has happened here,' said Harriet Hawk. 'The stupid mutt must've fallen off the treadmill again, then got up and just kept on marching. If it wasn't for that handrail, she would've marched right over the edge of the stairs. Turn her round, Dumbbell.'

Thank goodness, thought Lara as the big-eared giant grabbed her by the collar and pointed her away from the handrail, in the direction of the gym.

'But why did she turn through the door to the basement instead of marching straight ahead?' asked Squat, glaring at Lara suspiciously. 'Are you sure she's properly brainwashed?'

'What does it matter?' sneered Harriet Hawk. 'She's only a dog.'

'I dunno,' said Dumbbell. 'There's something odd about that mutt and her pups.'

Speak for yourself, big ears!

'What a pair of scaredy-cats,' sighed Harriet Hawk. She approached Lara and clicked her fingers in front of her face. Lara wasn't quite sure what to do so she took a guess and stopped. She stood, unblinking and hoping. *Does click mean stop?*

'See,' said Harriet Hawk. 'The mutt is totally gone.'

Phew! thought Lara as Dumbbell scooped up the heavy dog and plonked her back on the treadmill. She was soon marching again, acting out her zombie role perfectly.

'Besides,' Harriet Hawk added, 'even if she isn't quite zombified yet, this implant should sort her out!'

Before Lara could do anything, Harriet
Hawk whipped a syringe from Squat's tray and
jabbed it into her sticky-up ear. She just
managed not to yelp.

'Good,' said Harriet Hawk, withdrawing the
needle. 'The implant is under the skin now.
That's one down, twenty to go. Let's get injecting.'

Lara held her breath, waiting for the implant
to take over her mind, but nothing happened.
*Huh! That doesn't work on me either! Doggie brain-
waves rule!*

Harriet Hawk moved along the row, injecting
an implant into an ear lobe of each zombie-squad

member. 'That's this little batch sorted,' she said proudly. 'Now for the tricky part,' she said, holding up her crossed fingers. She pulled a small electronic device out of her pocket and pressed a red button. All the ear lobes started to glow with a blue light. An evil smile lit Harriet Hawk's lips. She lifted the device to her mouth and spoke. 'This is your captain speaking,' she said. 'You must obey my every word.'

Lara looked out of the corner of her eye as she marched. 'Obey every word,' chanted the adults.

'Hands on heads,' commanded Harriet Hawk.

Squat jumped up and down in excitement as the marching adults obeyed. He grabbed the gadget. 'Walk like a chicken,' he bellowed, almost collapsing as the marchers started clucking and waggling their elbows.

'Enough,' shouted Harriet Hawk, snatching the control back and glaring at Squat. 'This is not a laughing matter.'

'Not a laughing matter,' echoed the marching adults.

'In two days' time you will be part of my evil plan,' announced Harriet Hawk.

'Evil plan,' droned the adults, their ear lobes flashing blue.

'I mean *very* evil plan,' she smirked.

'*Very* evil plan,' chanted the army.

'*Very, very* evil plan,' piped up Squat, before he was cut down by another icy stare from his boss.

'Idiot,' Harriet Hawk snarled. She put her finger to her lips and then pressed the button once more. The ear lobes stopped flashing and the treadmills stopped. The adults stopped marching and stepped off the machines, looking a little confused.

'Well done, everyone,' said Harriet Hawk.

'Great workout. Back here tomorrow, please, same time. Until then, off you go.'

Obediently, the adults began to shuffle, exhausted, towards the door. 'Hurry them up, gentlemen,' ordered Harriet Hawk with a yawn. 'I'm holding the country to ransom in two days' time. I need my beauty sleep.'

You sure do, thought Lara, looking at Harriet Hawk over her shoulder as Dumbbell and Squat hustled everyone out of the gym. *About a thousand years of it!*

The last adult left the gym and Squat locked the door.

'Yeah! That was so easy!' Dumbbell high-fived Squat and then turned to Harriet Hawk, who gave him an icy and withering glare.

'I don't think so,' she sneered. 'But it's true, everything is going to plan. Eighty gyms recruited. That's nearly two thousand parents zombiefied and implanted.'

'All awaiting their orders,' grinned Squat.

'We'll test this local army tomorrow tonight,' she reminded him, holding up the small electronic device, her thumb hovering over the red button. 'And if it works, we'll switch on the big receiver and activate zombie armies across the land.'

'*When* it works, boss,' chuckled Dumbbell. 'I checked the radio mast when I was up on the roof. It's ready and waiting. As for these new recruits, they will act normally enough to carry on with their lives until you press the red button – but if any one of them tries to remember how they were brainwashed, the implant will send pain pulses into their brains to make them stop. It's a no-brainer,' he said, disappearing into peals of laughter at his own joke. 'Geddit?' he snorted. 'No brai . . .' his voice trailed off when he realized the other two weren't laughing.

'I have to say, ma'am, it's total genius,' leered Squat, sucking up to his boss.

Harriet Hawk looked down sternly at her henchman. '*Evil* genius,' she corrected.

'Well, dear, did you enjoy that?' asked Mrs Cook as they walked back home across the field.

'Yes, I did!' said Mr Cook. 'At least, I think so. I can't quite remember what we did, however much I try . . . Ouch!' He winced and gripped his head.

Lara looked back at the dark gym. She could see the radio mast on the flat roof. She noticed a light was fixed to the top of the mast, and began piecing the puzzle together.

I'm pretty sure, once that lights up, the zombie army will be called to action. She looked at Mr Cook nursing his throbbing head. *Poor man! There's no point me trying to tell him he's brainwashed; he'll just end up with an even bigger headache.*

'That's odd,' said Mrs Cook, opening their garden gate. 'I can't remember either.' She grimaced. 'Ooh! Ouch! Bit of a headache there for a minute.'

'One thing's for sure,' said Mr Cook. 'I can't wait to go back for our next gym session! I feel strangely drawn to Hawk's Gym.'

'Me too,' said Mrs Cook, pushing open the kitchen door. 'Let's see if Mrs Brown will babysit for us again tomorrow night.'

'I most certainly will not!' cried Mrs Brown.

Lara frowned. What was going on? Mrs Brown was standing in the kitchen with a sleeping Marmalade in her arms. The kitten had a bandage around his middle. Ben and Sophie were sitting at the table looking very upset.

'Whatever's the matter, Mrs Brown? Have the children been naughty?' asked Mr Cook.

'No. The children have been fine, but your pup attacked my poor Marmalade. So I'm afraid you'll have to find another babysitter from now on.'

Mrs Brown hurried out of the door. Mr and Mrs Cook followed her, full of apologies.

'Spud? Star?' woofed Lara. 'Where are you?'

The pups crept out from under the kitchen table. Spud ran to Lara and hid under her tum. He was trembling. 'Oh, Ma!' he whined. 'Mrs Brown thinks I bit Marmalade!'

'But he didn't,' whimpered Star, her eyes big with tears. 'Spud was so brave! He rescued Marmalade from a big eagle and then he carried him all the way home on his back!'

'I admit I was a bit jealous of the way everyone loved him, even Ollie. But I would never hurt him. You have to believe me, Ma!' whimpered Spud.

'I do believe you, Spud,' soothed Lara, licking Spud's ear. 'I've seen that eagle too. Harriet Hawk is his owner.'

'What's going on, Lara?' whispered Ben.

'*We* know Spud didn't hurt Marmalade,' added Sophie. 'But who, or what, did?'

'Let me explain,' woofed Lara, jumping up on to a chair and pulling Ben's notepad towards her. Spud and Star jumped up beside her and

Ben and Sophie leant closer. Lara picked up a thick felt-tip pen in her mouth and thought for a minute. There was so much to tell them, she was not sure where to begin!

I'd better start with Mr and Mrs Cook, she thought sadly. *Sophie and Ben deserve to know what's happening to their mum and dad – and I need to do it before Mr and Mrs Cook come back.* Gripping the pen more firmly in her mouth, Lara bent forward and began to write.

Ben and Sophie looked at each other, their brows furrowed. 'Zombies?' said Ben. 'The living dead?'

Lara shook her head. *Not exactly*, she thought. *At least, I don't think they're dead*.

'Ma, Dad, teacher, police. Grown-ups,' she scribbled, some slobber smudging her writing.

Spud was on his hind legs, his front paws out in front of him. 'Zombies,' he woofed, walking round the kitchen with his eyes bulging and his tongue lolloping.

'Hawk's Gym,' wrote Lara. 'Danger! Zombie army let loose in 2 days.'

Ben frowned. 'Sounds a bit far-fetched. Shall I tell Mum and Dad?'

Lara shook her head. *Definitely not*, she thought. *The pups and I will investigate and report back*.

'Ring Prof,' she scribbled.

Ben reached for his mobile and dialled a number in Chile.

11. Zombie Test

Lara staggered across the living room on stiff legs and collapsed on to the sofa.

She had just finished her final zombie-squad session at Hawk's Gym and everything ached. Mr and Mrs Cook were suffering too; after two days of intensive training, they were exhausted and covered in bruises. They had crawled upstairs to bed as soon as they got home.

'What was the training this time, Ma?' asked Star.

'Boxing and swimming,' Lara whimpered. 'Lots and lots of swimming.'

'What is she planning, Ma?' asked Star.

'I wish I knew but I can't get near the basement command centre. I did overhear Harriet Hawk say that tonight would be a final test before the big day tomorrow.'

'Maybe we could ask the prof to get a search warrant?' woofed Star.

'Ben left him a message,' sighed Lara. 'Fingers crossed he's on his way back from South America.'

'What about the police?' yapped Spud. 'We could get Ben or Sophie to call them.'

Lara shook her head. 'That won't work. The local bobby is one of the zombie squad! No, we're on our own, pups.'

'And so are they,' woofed Star, nodding towards the kitchen where Ben and Sophie were trying to wash their school shirts, do their homework and make tomorrow's packed lunches, all at the same time.

Lara sighed. 'Poor things. I have to sort this out, for their sakes. Zombie mums and dads are useless. They're desperate to get their real parents back.'

'Except him,' yapped Spud, as Ollie ran past clutching a can of fizzy drink and a big bar of chocolate. 'He's having a great time!'

Lara watched Ollie race to the top of the stairs and then slide down the banister, still clutching his drink and chocolate. Sophie and Ben had decided not to worry him by telling

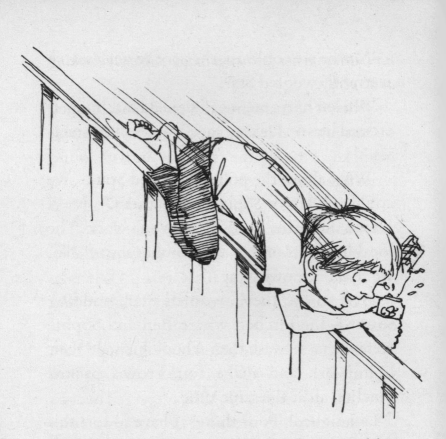

him about the brainwashed zombie squad his parents had joined; all he knew was that his mum and dad had suddenly stopped telling him what to do. He was staying up late, eating nothing but junk food and he hadn't had a bath for three days.

I wish Mrs Brown would come round and sort him out, thought Lara, before remembering that their next-door neighbour wasn't speaking to them. *Well, at least Marmalade's recovering. I saw him sitting on her kitchen window sill today, looking quite perky.*

Ollie raced back into the room and jumped on to the sofa. Picking up the remote control, he flicked through the channels until he found a zombie film. 'Cool!' he cried.

'He wouldn't say that if he knew he had two zombie parents upstairs,' Star yapped.

'He'll be sick if he eats that all by himself,' Spud said, drooling, as he watched Ollie take a big bite out of his chocolate bar. 'I'll help him out.'

'That's not how we help him out, Spud,' Lara said firmly. 'We help him out by getting him to bed before midnight.' She staggered over to the television and turned it off with her nose.

'I was watching that!' cried Ollie. 'It was an evil zombies film.'

In reply, Lara put on her sternest expression and pointed up the stairs with her paw. *Get some sleep*, she thought. *We might have to do battle with some real zombies tomorrow.*

Two hours later, Ollie was finally asleep, with Spud snoring beside him. Ben and Sophie had gone to bed too, and Star had snuggled down beside Sophie. Lara was the only one left awake. She was sitting at the kitchen table with a cup of cocoa, puzzling over a question that had been bothering her ever since the first night at the gym. Harriet Hawk had chosen her zombie squad after reading the membership forms everyone had filled in. What did those twenty hand-picked people have in common? She had tried and tried to figure it out, but she could not find a connection.

Lara yawned hugely and scrambled down from the kitchen chair. *One last check before I turn in.* She trotted around the ground floor of the house, making sure everything was switched off. In the hall, she went up on her hind legs and pressed a front paw against the light switch, wincing at her aching muscles. As the hall went dark, she heard a noise from the landing. Lara turned and felt her hackles rise. Two shadowy figures were coming down the stairs towards her.

The figures stepped into a beam of moonlight, and Lara saw that it was Mr and Mrs Cook. She gave a relieved sigh, but then she saw that they were both walking stiffly with their arms straight out in front of them. Their mouths were slack and their eyes were blank.

As they reached the hallway, Lara flattened herself against the wall to avoid being trodden on and they marched straight past her towards the front door.

Their earlobes are glowing! They're zombie-walking!

Mr Cook was wearing his favourite Superman pyjamas. Mrs Cook was in her pink nightdress. They were both barefoot but, when they reached the rows of shoes by the door, they stopped.

'Shooooes,' slurred Mr Cook.

'Shooooooes,' echoed Mrs Cook.

They both turned and shoved their feet into random items of footwear. Mr Cook squashed his right foot into a black, peep-toed high heel and his left foot into one of Sophie's roller boots. Mrs Cook ended up in a plastic garden clog and an oversized hiking boot.

Mr Cook looked very pleased with himself. 'Goooodshoooooes,' he moaned as he wobbled and slid along the hallway to the front door.

'Gooooood,' echoed Mrs Cook, clumping along behind him.

Mr Cook opened the door and the two of them stomped and wobbled down the garden path and into the street. They seemed to know where they were going.

They must've been summoned by Harriet Hawk, thought Lara as she eased the door shut behind her and trotted after them. *They're heading for the gym.*

It was after midnight and the village was quiet. At first, Mr and Mrs Cook stumbled along the empty streets alone, but then other members of the zombie squad appeared in ones and twos, and soon the whole group was shambling along together with their arms out in front of them and their eyes staring at nothing. They were all in nightclothes and wearing everything from dinosaur slippers to snowshoes on their feet. Lara walked stiffly with them, pretending to be hypnotized too.

When they all came to a sudden stop, Lara nearly cannoned into the zombie in front of her. *You need brake lights on your bum!* she thought as she skidded to a halt with her nose centimetres from his stripy pyjamas.

As though they had been given an order, the zombie squad all turned smartly to the right. Lara turned with them and saw that they were in front of the school.

Why have they stopped here? The gym's much further down the road, by the playing fields.

Until now the zombie squad had walked in eerie silence, but as they marched through the school gates and up the drive, they began to chant one word over and over again. 'Destroy! Destroy! Destroy!'

Lara looked around frantically as she marched beside them. *What do I do? I can't let them destroy the school! Ben, Sophie and Ollie love it here!*

But the zombie squad never reached the

building. At the top of the drive they turned left and headed for the school allotment. That was when Lara spotted three dark figures standing on the grass. One had ears like cup handles, one had no neck at all and the third had a hooked, beak-like nose. Dumbbell, Squat – and Harriet Hawk.

I knew you'd be around somewhere, Lara thought. *After all, you're the puppet master, pulling the strings to make this lot dance.*

Lara caught a glint of teeth in the moonlight. Harriet Hawk was smiling. 'Phase one of our test-run successfully completed,' she crowed. 'They came when they were called. Now let's see if they will follow my orders and destroy the allotment.'

Lara gasped. Why did Harriet Hawk want her zombie squad to destroy the allotment? Things were getting more and more puzzling.

Trouble's on the way, she thought. *Mr and Mrs Cook won't obey this order. They know how much work Ben, Sophie and Ollie have put into growing these vegetables.*

But she was wrong. Mr and Mrs Cook waded in with the rest of the zombie squad. Lara stared, horrified, as they pulled down beanpoles, pulled up carrots and trampled on lettuces. Harriet Hawk had them well and truly brainwashed.

'That mutt isn't joining in,' growled Squat.

Lara gulped as twenty zombie heads turned her way. The zombie squad glared at her for a few seconds and then everyone, including Mr and Mrs Cook, dropped the mangled vegetables they were holding, raised their arms and reeled towards her, twitching their outstretched fingers. 'Destroy!'

Lara froze. *Zombie attack! My worst nightmare! If I join in with trashing the allotment, they'll think I'm one of them and leave me alone. But the children have worked so hard! I can't obliterate Ollie's onions, or batter Ben's beetroots, or even shred Sophie's spinach, although personally I can't stand the stuff . . .*

The zombie squad lurched closer. Their fingers reached for her. Quickly, she selected a patch of soil in the far corner of the allotment where only weeds were growing. 'Destroy!' she barked, digging down into the soil with her front paws. 'Destroy!'

The zombie squad stopped. Their neck bones clicked as they all tilted their heads to watch her. Would they be fooled? After a long

moment, they turned back to their own digging and Lara gave a sigh of relief. *Phew! From Spy Dog to zombie dog. I deserve a pooch Oscar for that performance.*

Shifting her position so that her rear end was pointing at Harriet Hawk, Lara stood over the pile of earth she had dug up and scrabbled at it with her front paws. A hail of mud and thistles flew out from between her back legs and sprayed all over the three baddies. *Bullseye! That's for Ben, Sophie and Ollie.*

'Stop!' spluttered Harriet Hawk.

Lara stopped. So did the rest of the zombie squad. They stood there in the mud with blank faces, waiting for their next order. Lara copied them, trying not to look too pleased as she watched Harriet Hawk picking lumps of mud out of her hair.

'Well, that proves it, boss,' said Squat. 'Your little test has worked. They're zombies all right. Although I'm still not sure about that ugly mutt,' he muttered, giving Lara a suspicious glare.

Me ugly? Have you looked in the mirror lately, chum?

'Zombified is the word, Squat.' Harriet Hawk smiled her cold smile. 'If they had any control left over their own minds, they wouldn't have destroyed their own children's vegetable allotment.'

Lara stifled a gasp. *That's the connection! The people in the zombie squad all have children at this school!*

'I still don't get it,' said Dumbbell. He swept his arm across the destroyed allotment. 'Why is it good that they did this?'

'Because it shows that they will hurt their children when I order them to,' explained Harriet Hawk.

Lara let out a low growl before she could

stop herself. *Harriet Hawk is going to make Mr and Mrs Cook hurt Ben, Sophie and Ollie!* She just managed to stop her upper lip from curling up into a snarl as Squat gave her another suspicious look. *But how will that make her into one of the richest, most powerful women in the world? I have to find out – and fast!*

'Go back to your homes, zombie squad,' Harriet Hawk ordered. 'Meet me at the gym tomorrow morning after your children have gone to school. It's time to unleash my master plan!'

Time is running out, thought Lara as she shambled away with the zombie squad. *I must find a way into that command centre tomorrow. Whatever it takes.*

12. Fatal Attraction

It had been a very odd morning in the Cook household. Mr and Mrs Cook had woken up covered in dried mud and there was a trail of muddy footprints leading from the front door to their bedroom. Every time they tried to remember how they had got that way, they had been hit by painful headaches. Once they had cleaned themselves up, they had sat silently at the kitchen table, looking bewildered and clutching cups of coffee, while Ben and Sophie had raced around, getting themselves and Ollie ready for school. Lara had longed for the cheerful chaos of a normal school day.

The Cooks didn't seem to want to move from the table so Lara and the pups walked the children to school. Lara knew that now was the time that the zombie mums and dads had

been ordered back to the gym, so on the way back she made Star and Spud hide with her in a nearby hedge as twenty members of the zombie squad straggled in through the doors of Hawk's Gym. The midnight destruction of the school vegetable allotment had taken its toll on them. They were all pale and bruised, their hands were covered in cuts and scratches, and some of them, Mr Cook included, were limping.

Lara winced in sympathy. She knew that Mr Cook had a blister the size of a plum on his heel. *That's what happens when you go for a walk in a black high-heeled shoe, four sizes too small for you.*

'What shall we do, Ma?' yapped Star as the last of the zombies made their way into the gym.

'Harriet Hawk said that today's the day. So

I'll play-act being part of the zombie gang and work as an insider. See if there's a way into the command room.'

'And we can work our way round the outside looking for another entrance,' suggested Star.

Lara nodded. 'Don't do anything dangerous, though.'

'Don't worry, Ma. We'll find a way in. A fire door, an open window, even an air vent,' yapped Star eagerly. 'We're only pups; we can squeeze through the tiniest spaces.'

Lara gave Spud's fat tum a doubtful glance.

'That's all muscle,' woofed Spud, looking offended.

'You're looking a lot slimmer, Ma,' said Star.

Lara glanced down at herself and was surprised to see that Star was right – she had lost her pooch paunch.

'Well, at least Hawk's Gym is good for something,' she woofed. 'Or maybe it's all the worrying I've been doing. I'd better head inside now before anyone notices I'm not with the parents. I hope we can find out what Harriet Hawk is planning; I have a feeling time is running out.'

'We'll do our best, Ma,' woofed Spud and Star.

'I know you will,' barked Lara. 'I'm very proud of you both. Look after each other!'

Harriet Hawk was looking extra pleased. Practice runs were over. Today was to be the real thing.

The zombies stood in the gym, ears glowing, awaiting their next instructions. Lara stood with them, being careful to stay absolutely still. Her eyes moved right and she watched Harriet Hawk punch a number into the keypad on the control-room door. She memorized the number, then her eyes quickly reverted straight ahead as Harriet Hawk glanced at the assembled crowd before disappearing through the door with her henchmen.

Lara knew she had no choice. *I have to find out what's going on in that room*, she thought as she broke from the crowd and approached the metal door, sniffing intently, her ears pricked for danger. She jumped up on to her hind legs and punched the numbers into the lock. There was a beep as the lock lifted and she nosed her way through into the gym's nerve centre.

Lara tiptoed down the metal staircase and crouched under a table. The room was full of

laptops and huge video screens. Harriet Hawk, Dumbbell and Squat were huddled over one particular screen. Lara's sticky-up ear was on full alert.

'Let's get this thing moving,' she heard Harriet Hawk say. 'Summon the children. It's showtime!'

Spud and Star stayed hidden until Lara had disappeared inside the gym.

'Ready to go, bro?' whispered Star.

Spud swallowed and glanced around uneasily. 'In a minute.'

'What's the problem?'

'No problem,' said Spud bravely. 'But let's keep our heads down, just in case.' He began to commando-crawl through the grass towards the gym.

Star could see that Spud was worried about something. 'We'll be fine,' she woofed as she crawled alongside him. 'We've fought baddies before and always come out on top.'

'It's not Squat and Dumbbell I'm bothered about,' admitted Spud. 'We can outrun those two muscle-heads any day. But we can't outrun that big bird.' He glanced up at the flat roof of the gym. 'Do you think it can see us right now?' he whispered, with a shiver.

'Harriet Hawk puts a hood over its head during the day, probably to keep it calm. I'm sure we'll be fine,' assured Star, her words more confident than her thoughts.

'You're right, sis.' Spud's tail began to wag and he set off at a steady trot with his tail held high. 'We're highly trained Spy Pups. Let's get stuck into this adventure.'

Star shook her head as she followed him. 'Brothers,' she sighed.

The puppies made it as far as the side wall of the gym, checking for unlocked doors or open windows, when Star came to a halt.

'Did you hear that?' she whispered, rotating her sticky-up ear like a radar dish.

'Was it that bird?' yelped Spud, looking up at the sky.

'No. It sounded like children. Lots of them.'

'Yes, I hear them now,' woofed Star. 'And Mr Thompson, I think.'

The school teacher appeared first, his ear lobe glowing, his eyes glazed and his feet plodding purposefully towards Hawk's Gym. Twenty children scurried behind, the little ones struggling to keep up.

'Slow down, Mr T,' panted Ollie, lagging towards the back.

'Your parents need you,' droned the teacher. 'They are in great danger.'

The pups peered at the strange crowd.

'It's not only the parents that are in danger,' woofed Spud. 'Mr Thompson is leading the kids into the thick of it.'

'But they can't go into Hawk's Gym,' woofed Spud. 'It'll be like entering the lion's den.'

'The zombies' den,' gulped Star. 'And I think zombies might be even worse than lions. We have to turn them back!'

The pups raced across the field and skidded to a halt in front of Ben, Sophie and Ollie.

'Stop!' yapped Spud, holding up his front paws. 'It's too dangerous!'

'Out of the way, pups,' ordered Ben. 'We're going in to rescue our parents! Lara told us that something weird is going on at the gym. And Mr Thompson says they're in terrible danger. He says they're asking for us.'

'Yes,' agreed Sophie. 'They've been acting like zombies since they joined Hawk's Gym. And all our friends are saying the same about their parents. And we want to find out what's got into them.'

'But that's just it!' yelped Star. 'They're not your parents when they're in that gym. Harriet Hawk has them so zombified, she could even order them to turn on you!'

'Sorry, Star – I can guess what you're saying, but you won't stop us,' said Sophie. 'I want my mum and dad back.'

'Me too,' said Ollie. 'I don't want to watch scary films any more. Or eat any more chocolate. And I want to be told to have a bath, and brush my teeth, and go to bed. A-and I want a cuddle.'

For a moment all the children were quiet, thinking about the cuddles they were missing. Then their sad expressions were replaced with looks of fierce determination.

'Uh-oh,' yapped Spud as the children lifted their heads and glared at Hawk's Gym. 'Nothing's going to stop them now!'

Lara remained under the table, hardly daring to breathe. She didn't need to watch the action because Squat was doing a fantastic commentary of what he could see on the big screen.

'Mr Thompson is announcing it to the children,' he grunted. 'And here they come. Like kids to a candy shop.'

'Zombie shop,' giggled Dumbbell.

They watched as the children followed their teacher, pied-piper style, towards the gym.

'Our hostages,' purred Harriet Hawk. 'This is even easier than I thought it would be.'

Hostages? thought Lara, still trying to piece the bits together. *I'm still not quite sure what she's doing but the more I discover, the worse it gets!*

Lara peered out from under the table and caught a glimpse of the screen. She saw Mr Thompson striding towards the front entrance of the gym, a string of children close behind. Her heart sank.

Not good! Everyone I love most in the world, all under one roof with a dangerous super-baddie! Think,

Lara, think. This is going to need all my Spy Dog powers!

Harriet Hawk and her henchmen seemed satisfied. 'The children are here. Make sure the pool is secure,' purred Harriet Hawk. Squat switched off the TV and the three baddies returned to the gym. Lara crept after them, her heart pounding and her mind racing

Mr Thompson was first into the gym, the children following behind.

'Welcome, young ones,' began Harriet Hawk. 'Come to save your parents? How very noble.'

'What have you done to them?' demanded Ben, pointing at the adults standing in a large blue hole in the ground where the swimming pool used to be. 'And why are their earlobes flashing?'

'Come here, children,' droned the parents in unison, holding out their arms for an awkward zombie hug.

Sophie's best friend immediately ran towards the empty pool and clambered down the silver ladder to join her mum. The rest of the children followed, including Ben, Sophie and Ollie, until the blue rectangle was filled with children and their emotionless parents. Ollie looked up at his mum who stared blankly ahead. He jumped up and down waving his hands in front of her face.

Lara watched, a puzzled expression on her doggy face. Netball posts had been left round the edge of the empty pool. Dumbbell and Squat appeared with armfuls of cable and wound them round the posts, quickly fencing off the pool so it looked like a sunken wrestling ring.

'What are you doing?' shouted Ben.

'Making you secure,' purred Harriet Hawk. She looked down at the children, who stared back, confused. She nodded to Squat, who disappeared into the control room. A low hum began and the cables started to glow. Squat returned and threw a tennis ball at the cables – it exploded in a ball of fire. He smiled and gave a thumbs up to his boss.

'Squat, if you would be so kind,' she said.

Squat lumbered over to a large red wheel on the wall and started to turn it. Water erupted from the middle of the pool.

'It's filling up,' began Sophie, making for one of the ladders.

'Bad idea,' yelled Harriet Hawk, pointing to the smouldering tennis ball. 'Didn't your zombie teacher tell you anything in science? The cables are electrified. And everyone knows that water and electricity don't mix.'

Sophie stared up at the woman, her bottom lip trembling. 'So we can't get out?'

'And the water's getting higher,' said Ollie. 'I've got my ten-metres badge, but what happens when it gets deep?'

Harriet Hawk said nothing, her evil eyes and upturned lips saying it all.

Ben looked at the rising water, now around his knees. 'Mum. Dad. Help us,' he yelled, panic rising in his voice. He slapped his dad hard in the face but there was no reaction. Ollie thought it looked like good fun so he had a go too.

Harriet Hawk moved as close to the electric cables as she dared and peered into the rising tide of people. 'Today is a very special day,' she beamed. 'After years of planning and preparation, my master plan finally goes into action.'

She picked up a remote control, switched on all the big screens around the gym and pointed at the screens. 'Men and women are pounding on treadmills in my gyms all around the country. I've brainwashed them all. Eighty zombie squads in place, all made up of parents with children at the local schools. My brainwashed beauties. I call them my zombie army!'

'Their ears are flashing too!' cried Sophie.

Harriet Hawk couldn't help smiling. 'I made sure all my gyms were built only a few minutes' walk from the schools. When the signal starts transmitting from the radio mast up on the roof here, it will activate the implant every zombie squad member has under the skin of their earlobes. The treadmills will stop and the marching will begin.'

'Marching where?' shouted Ben, his panic rising as fast as the water.

'To the schools, of course,' cackled the evil woman. 'To collect their children and put them in mortal danger. Total genius,' she smiled.

'Total insanity,' yelled Ben. 'Lara! Where are you? We need you!'

Harriet Hawk looked around for the dog but Lara was nowhere to be seen.

'Your cowardly dog seems to have done a runner,' sneered Harriet Hawk. There's only one person who can help you now . . .'

13. Prime Minister's Questions

Harriet Hawk beckoned to Dumbbell and he clicked open the camcorder. 'Time to record my message to Number 10,' she chirped as Hercules the eagle settled on her shoulder. She smoothed her eyebrows and glanced at the lens. 'How do I look?'

'Like a pirat–' began Dumbbell, before being jabbed in the ribs by his cauliflower-faced colleague.

'Beautiful, boss,' Squat lied.

'I know! And soon I'll be rich and powerful too!'

'Us too, boss,' said Dumbbell, his big ears practically flapping with excitement.

'Quite,' said Harriet Hawk. 'Rich enough to get some ear surgery perhaps. Now be quiet and listen to me make my ransom demand.'

Dumbbell pointed the camcorder at his boss and she composed herself before he grinned and gave the thumbs up.

'Hello, Prime Minister. Indeed, hello, nation. I am Harriet Hawk. But then you probably already know that.' A vain smile lit her lips and she reached up and stroked Hercules. 'I have a little home movie to show you. As you can see, the parents in my zombie army are holding their *own* children hostage in my gymnasium.'

She paused while Dumbbell panned across the gym, zooming in on Ollie who was hanging on to Ben's shoulders and kicking with his feet. The water continued to rise. Dumbbell kept a steady hand and returned to Harriet Hawk's beaky face.

'This is a little tester. Just a handful of children. I'm sure you don't want innocent children to suffer, Prime Minister. That would look terribly bad in the morning newspapers.'

Harriet Hawk left what she thought was a dramatic pause before continuing in a business-like manner. 'So you get the chance to play hero! And get yourself re-elected! It's *deadly* simple. All you have to do is transfer a billion pounds to my bank account. But I'm a generous person, Prime Minister, so I'm giving you thirty minutes. If I get my billion pounds, you have my word that the children will be released. If I don't, then I will activate a signal and this scene will be repeated in eighty gyms across the country.' Harriet Hawk reached up and stroked her eagle, leaving time for the information to sink in. 'That's a lot of little children,' she emphasized, cocking her head to one side and doing her best innocent smile.

The face disappeared, replaced by another sixty seconds of the swirling pool full of panic-stricken children and emotionless parents, all swimming for their lives. Ollie managed a heroic shout of 'Don't do it, Your Highness,' before the camera swung back to Harriet Hawk's evil face.

'And no rescue attempts or I activate my army immediately,' she said icily. She held her watch to the camera and tapped it. 'Twenty-nine minutes and counting,' she threatened as Dumbbell zoomed in on her eyes. 'Twenty-nine minutes to save the world.'

Dumbbell clicked Pause and gave another thumbs up. 'In the can,' he grinned, tapping the camcorder lovingly.

Harriet Hawk returned Hercules to his perch

and placed the small black hood back on to his
head. She took the camcorder and ejected the
memory card, handing it to Squat.

'Get this uploaded,' she purred. 'And, Dumbbell, you watch for signs of rescue.'

'You can't do this,' gurgled Ben, struggling
to stay afloat while holding on to Ollie.

Harriet Hawk smirked. 'But I already am,
dear boy.'

The evil lady swooped towards the control

room and was punching in the code when Dumbbell yelled out. 'There are those puppies!' He pointed at one of the CCTV screens. 'Looks like they're trying to break in. It might be an attempted rescue, boss.'

Harriet Hawk huffed in frustration as pictures of Star and Spud snuffling round the boundaries of the gym played out in front of her. She'd noticed that the big dog had gone missing and now these little dogs were making a nuisance of themselves too. Years of planning had gone into getting this far. There was no way she would let dogs ruin it. She calmly sauntered over to the corner of the room, put on the big black leather glove and removed the hood from her eagle. Hercules climbed on to her arm

'I'm taking Hercules out to play,' she declared. 'He's been waiting to get revenge on those two ever since they sabotaged his night-time hunt.'

'Hercules, darling,' she cooed to the eagle on her arm, as she headed up the stairs to the roof. 'It's suppertime.'

Harriet Hawk had completely missed the sticky-up ear poking from the wet-towel bin behind her. Lara nosed her head out of the bin, sniffing the air. Squat was uploading the video and Harriet Hawk was making her way on to the roof terrace.

That just leaves one baddie, Lara thought, glancing at Dumbbell who was occupied with watching the CCTV images of the pups.

Lara's muzzle wrinkled as she tried to concentrate on the best rescue plan.

The water had risen so high that even the bigger children were now having to swim. The frazzled tennis ball meant they were too scared to hang on to the metal bar at the side of the pool.

And it's a fitness pool, Lara thought. *So there's no shallow end*. Ollie was hanging on to his big brother's back, his legs kicking froggy-style. Lara had to admit Harriet Hawk's dastardly plan was rather clever. *On the evil scale, it's a ten*.

With Dumbbell still distracted by the pups, Lara crept out. Ben saw her and stifled a squeal of hope. But the villain heard him and swung round.

Lara bared her teeth and growled.

Dumbbell took a step towards Lara, grabbing a pool-cleaning net and jabbing it at her. Thinking quickly, Lara suddenly remembered the ball of llama-spit formula the professor had given her. Backing away from Dumbbell, she released the ball from her collar. It broke open, spilling a puddle of ultra-slippery gunk. Lara reached the edge of the pool, her backside nearly touching the electric cable. She felt the warm buzz of the current and the faint whiff of singed fur.

Yikes! That's as far as I go!

'Careful, Lara,' shouted Sophie, treading water as the pool water rose higher.

Come and get me, Mr Baddie, thought the retired Spy Dog, lowering her growl and trying to entice Dumbbell. *Just a few more steps and you're in the llama spit*. Dumbbell sprinted towards Lara, the cleaning net pointed at her. He picked up speed – and hit the world's slipperiest poolside.

The man was helpless. He slid on his feet, his arms hanging on to the long pole to keep balance, but there was no stopping him. He was heading straight for the cables and Lara saw horror on Dumbbell's face as he remembered the frazzled tennis ball. In desperation, the man managed to hook the net in one of the pool steps and he pole-vaulted the top cable. Lara and the children watched as he sailed through the air and landed with a splash in the pool.

He surfaced, flapping and spluttering. 'Get
me out of here,' yelled Dumbbell. 'I'm a
rubbish swimmer!'

'You should have done your ten metres like
me,' smiled Ollie, holding on to his brother's
shoulder with one hand and splashing water in
the man's face with the other.

One down, thought Lara. *Two to go!*

★

Squat heard the commotion and burst through the metal door, fury on his face. His anger deepened as he saw his partner-in-crime sploshing around in the pool.

'How on earth did you get in there, idiot?' he yelled, the veins sticking out on his neck.

'It was that blasted dog,' gurgled Dumbbell.

'Spy Dog actually,' corrected Ollie, almost enjoying himself.

Squat looked round anxiously. Lara was standing near the towel bin, hackles raised and lip curled. He glanced back at his colleague. 'Well, you're stuck for a while. If I switch the leccy off, then they'll all escape. Tread water. The video is uploading,' he said to his mate. 'I'll take care of the dog.'

14. Angry Bird

Spud and Star were scraping at the earth round the drain when they heard screeching above them.

'Dinner time,' yelped Star.

'I don't think so,' yapped Spud. 'We've not had lunch yet.'

'Not for us, silly! It's dinner time for the angry bird coming our way!'

The pups flung themselves sideways. A second later, the huge eagle shot over their heads, screaming with hunger.

'I hate that bird!' barked Spud as they scrambled to their feet.

'Go and catch yourself some breakfast, Hercules!' shouted Harriet Hawk from the gym roof. 'You haven't been fed since yesterday so I know they won't escape you.'

The bird of prey soared high, fixing its eagle eyes on the puppies.

Star looked around. They were surrounded by open fields and although the grass was quite long she was sure they'd be spotted from above.

'The hedge!' she yapped. 'That's our only cover. Go, go, go, bro!'

The pups began to run, but they had only gone a few metres when a shadow loomed over them again. Spud shuddered with fear, remembering what the eagle's talons had done to poor Marmalade. He was slower than his sister and was carrying more meat so would make a tastier eagle meal. Spud heard the rush of huge wings and, in his panic, tripped over his own paws. He was up and running again a second later, but he was sure that his tumble had cost him his life. The eagle was directly over his head now, and was too good a hunter to miss such an easy target.

A fat puppy in an open field in broad daylight. At least Star will make it, he thought, his legs pumping but his shoulders tensed, waiting for the kill.

Bam! Star beamed her darkness torch directly into the eagle's face. The huge bird had gone

from light to night in
less than a second. It
was too late to pull out
of its dive and the bird
slammed into the grass
beside Spud.

'Yikes,' the puppy
yelped, sprinting for
his life. 'A very near miss.'

'Thank the prof for that,' barked Star. 'But
keep running. The eagle's down but not out.'

Behind Spud, the bird rose into the air again
and took off after Star. The eagle clearly now
wanted revenge. Star
shot a frightened look
over her shoulder
before fleeing for the
cover of the hedge as fast
as her short legs would
go.

Spud scrambled to his feet.
The eagle was gaining on Star.
'Go left, sis!' he howled.

Star beamed her torch into the
eagle's eyes again. She sprang sideways into a rabbit hole and yelped

as the eagle slammed into the grass where she had been only an instant earlier.

'Tunnel down as far as you can,' woofed Spud.

Star did not need to be told. She scrambled down, her ears pricked, listening for the bird. The eagle reached its head into the hole and pecked viciously into the dark. Star squeezed further down the hole, narrowly avoiding the attack as earth crumbled around her where Hercules' razor-sharp beak hit the tunnel.

Suddenly the eagle withdrew and flew up into the sky once more. Spud looked up into the sun. He was dazzled. Hercules had disappeared.

Could it be that he's given up? he thought. 'You OK, sis?' yapped the puppy.

'Fine, thanks,' came the muffled reply from deep within the rabbit hole. Star's nose peeped out and her whiskers twitched as she sniffed for signs of the eagle. Gradually her face appeared and she heard Spud woof with delight.

'He's gone, sis,' yapped her brother. 'We've defeated that ugly old bir—'

Spud felt the wind being knocked out of him

as the eagle swooped down and sank its talons into his plump body. He heard Star howling in anguish as he was carried high into the sky.

15. The Signal

Harriet Hawk put her binoculars to her eyes and watched as Hercules swooped to pick up one of the puppies. 'A starter for my hungry boy,' she smiled. She focused on the struggling puppy and noticed he was quite round. 'Or maybe you've gone straight for the main course,' she cackled.

Lowering her binoculars, she reached for her walkie-talkie. 'Squat,' she barked. 'Progress report.'

Squat's deep voice crackled out of the walkie-talkie. 'All prisoners swimming for their lives,' he said. 'You gave the PM thirty minutes, ma'am,' he added. 'But by the look of some of the younger kids, that might be a bit too long.'

'Excellent,' came the reply. 'A few early casualties will show we mean business.' Harriet

Hawk was enjoying herself. 'In fact,' she shrieked into the walkie-talkie, 'let's bring the whole plan forward. We've got a much better chance of the PM depositing a billion pounds if we mobilize our entire army.' There was stunned silence at the other end of the walkie-talkie. 'Did you hear me, dimwit?' she shouted. 'Over.'

'Erm, yes, boss,' replied Squat. 'But you told the prime minister he had thirty minutes.'

'Well, clearly, I lied,' shouted the woman into the walkie-talkie. 'I'm an evil villain,' she said proudly. 'So I'm allowed to lie. We're ready for the final part of our master plan.

Please activate the signal and unleash the army. Go down to the command centre and switch it on. You remember the secret password, don't you?'

'Yes, boss. It's –'

'The SECRET password, I said!'

'Sorry, boss. I'll sort it straight away.' The muscle man kept a wary eye on Lara as he hurried to the steel door and punched in the code. The door swung open and he clattered down the metal steps into the control room.

Lara watched him disappear. She considered her options.

Follow the baddie into the control room? Visit the roof to take out Harriet Hawk?

She looked into the pool. The children were tiring. One or two of the parents seemed to be struggling to stay afloat. She was snapped out of her thoughts when Squat returned, walkie-talkie in hand.

'Mission accomplished,' he said.

Squat held the walkie-talkie away from his ear as the gym was lit up by a cackling Harriet Hawk. 'It's working,' she squealed. 'I'm on the roof. I can see the light flashing. The transmitter is working.'

Lara looked up at the numerous TV screens to see the other zombie squads, ear lobes flashing, leaving the gyms and marching to the schools. She knew it wouldn't be long until they were crashing through the school gates to get their hands on the children.

Squat grinned when he saw what was happening on the screens. 'Watch them go!'

'Won't the teachers stop them?' shouted Ben.

'They know the parents,' spluttered Dumb-bell, struggling to stay afloat next to him. 'And they won't expect them to harm their own children. By the time the teachers realize what's really happening, it will be too late.'

Harriet Hawk's voice crackled over the walkie-talkie. 'I do believe that my little Hercules has caught himself a main course of puppy steak. Looks like my doggie problem is sorted out here. Can you please make sure you sort out the big doggie mess in there? Over.'

Lara's heart sank as Squat reached for a baseball bat. He stared menacingly at the dog. 'Over and out.'

16. Queen Kong

Think, Lara, think! She looked down at the struggling swimmers. *Not good!* The Spy Dog knew the only way to stop the plan was to turn off the signal. *And that means getting to the top of the tower. And then there's him*, she thought, raising her hackles at Squat.

The man held the baseball bat in one hand, slapping it into the palm of his other hand. 'I have the bat. You can be the ball.'

Lara looked around frantically, hoping a plan would form in her mind. She spied the steam room and bolted for the door, nosing it open. Steam billowed out and she heard the door slam behind her. A few seconds later it re-opened and Squat came in. Lara's lungs choked and her eyes burnt.

Why on earth do humans pay for this treatment?

she thought. Visibility was worse than the foggiest of mornings. Lara's keen ears picked out the man's footsteps and the bat slapping into his hand. She circled to the left, lost in the mist. 'Come here, doggy,' coaxed the man. 'I mean no harm.'

You big fat liar! Lara thought, crouching low, ready to pounce.

'There's only one way in and out, poochie,' said the man.

That's exactly why I lured you in here.

Squat wandered deeper into the steam room, one hand wafting away the mist.

Now, thought Lara, springing at the man.

She sank her teeth into his thigh and the steam room became a scream room. The bat came down full force but Squat had lost his focus through the pain and missed Lara, hitting the floor. Lara darted past him and out through the door. She slid the bolt into place and watched as the man hammered on the small steamed-up window. Lara could hear his muffled shouting. 'Let me out, you stupid animal,' he yelled, his fists banging hard. 'Let me out!'

Stupid animal? considered Lara. *Think again.*

I'm out here and you're the one trapped in there. Lara
turned the thermostat to Max. *Full steam ahead,*
she thought as she bounded up the stairs
towards the roof terrace. *I have to stop the signal!*

Harriet Hawk dropped her binoculars as Lara
burst through the door on to the roof terrace
and hurled herself at the radio tower.

'Get away from my tower, you mutt!' she
yelled, clip-clopping across the stone terrace
and leaping at the dog.

Lara scrambled up the metal bars of the tower
mast, hanging her front paws over the bars and
gripping them with her mouth to haul herself
up as fast as she could.

'Come down from there, you crazy pooch!' screeched Harriet Hawk, leaping up at Lara. 'I see what's happened here,' she panted as she began to climb up behind her. 'The brainwashing was too much for you. It's fried your tiny doggie brain.'

My brain's in perfect working order, thought Lara, swinging her front paw to the next level and heaving herself up. *But it's so frustrating having paws! No grip!* She looked down and saw Harriet Hawk rapidly closing the gap between them. *She's gaining!*

Harriet Hawk had got the hang of climbing. Spurred by adrenaline and the fear of seeing her evil dream slipping away, she reached upwards and grabbed Lara's back leg. She tugged and Lara nearly fell. The ex-Spy Dog kicked out and landed a well-practised blow on the lady's nose. There was a scream from below but Lara didn't have time to look. Her eyes were fixed on the flashing red light and the aerial at the top of the tower.

I have to stop the signal!

Lara felt the radio mast shake. Harriet Hawk was climbing up the tower like King Kong climbing up the side of the Empire State Building.

Clamping her aching jaws round the next strut, Lara struggled on, determined to get to the top, but the radio mast was beginning to creak and sway. Lara heard a crack as something snapped. Her heart raced as she realized, reaching out for the flashing red light at exactly the same time as Harriet Hawk, that the weight of two bodies was too much for the fragile structure to take. They were in danger of crashing to the ground at any moment.

Hercules was well trained. And he was very loyal to his owner. Harriet Hawk had taken care of him since he was a chick. As far as Hercules was concerned, Harriet Hawk was 'Mummy'. And the one thing he really loved was her outstretched arm. It was her calling card. The rules were clear. An outstretched arm meant a safe place to land and, if he'd been a good bird, he was rewarded with some raw steak.

Hercules was bored with looking for the other puppy and, besides, the wriggling one he was carrying was getting heavy. And there, at the top of the tower, was his mum's outstretched arm and the possibility of some raw steak. Hercules stopped flapping and started his descent. Tail feathers tucked in, eyes focused, he zoomed for home. Lara saw the eagle coming but Harriet Hawk hadn't a clue. The eagle opened its claws as it homed in on Harriet's arm. Spud fell towards the tower and the eagle landed on Harriet's arm.

The evil lady was already off balance when the bird hit. She screamed as Hercules flapped his huge wings and tried to settle. Harriet Hawk lost her grip and tumbled down the radio mast, bouncing off the gym roof and landing in a prickly hedge below.

Ouch, thought Lara. *That's going to hurt!*

Lara looked up and there was Spud, deposited at the top of the tower, balancing precariously on his round little tummy.

'Hi, Ma!' He waved weakly. 'Fancy seeing you up here!'

Lara did a double take. 'Hit that light, son!' she woofed. 'Stop the signal!'

Spud didn't need asking twice. He thumped his rear end against the glass and it fell to the floor. He took the aerial in his jaws and expertly snapped it in half.

'I think we've done it, Spud,' woofed Lara. 'I think we might just have saved all those children.'

Spud's tail wagged so hard he nearly fell from the tower. 'Don't underestimate it, Ma,' he woofed. 'I reckon we might just have saved the world!'

By the time the professor and his secret service agents arrived the electric current had been switched off and terrified parents were yanking their exhausted children from the pool. Lara and the pups had made their way back into the gym and were wagging hard.

'They're coming round!' woofed Star. 'No more flashing ear lobes.'

Mr and Mrs Cook hauled Ollie out. They shook their heads and blinked.

'What . . .?' said Mr Cook.

'Where . . .?' said Mrs Cook.

'Mum! Dad!' yelled Ben, Sophie and Ollie. 'You're back!'

'What are you doing down there?' cried Mrs Cook. 'Get out of that water this minute, before you catch your death!'

Ben laughed. 'You don't know how true that nearly was, Mum!'

As Ben and Sophie clambered out with the

help of their dad, Mrs Cook pulled the three of them in for an enormous hug.

Ollie squeezed his mum back tightly. He'd been waiting days for that cuddle.

Sophie noticed Spud was hurt. She ran to him, squeezing the puppy a little too tightly. 'You OK, little guy?' she asked, her eyes watering as she examined his cuts.

Spud wagged hard. 'Just a few scratches,' he barked bravely. 'From an angry bird.'

Star wagged harder and she jabbed a paw at the handcuffed mastermind of the gang. 'And there's Hawk,' she yapped. 'Another very angry bird.'

The hook-nosed woman shook her fist at Lara and the puppies. 'I'd have got away with it,' she scowled, 'if it wasn't for you meddling mutts.'

17. Tea with the PM

The prime minister stood stiffly in the middle of the Cooks' back garden. Professor Cortex stood next to him, pink-faced with pride and, on the prime minister's other side, an aide held a red velvet cushion with three medals resting on it.

Lara, Spud and Star were facing the prime minister, and the Cook family stood behind them, along with Agents T and K, and Mrs Brown from next door. Marmalade was curled up in her arms, licking his paws and pretending to be bored. Ollie had wandered off to inspect the prime minister's helicopter.

'This is Lara, sir,' said Professor Cortex. 'Or, to use her Spy Dog name, GM451.'

Lara stood to attention as the prime minister took one of the medals from the cushion and bent down to pin it to her new collar. 'For canine bravery and services to the nation,' he said as he straightened up again. 'Your country owes you a great debt, Spy Dog.'

Don't mention it, thought Lara, bringing up her front paw in a salute. She watched proudly as the prime minister pinned medals to Spud and Star's collars too. The little crowd clapped and cheered, and even Marmalade gave a few miaows.

Ollie had never seen a helicopter in real life before. He walked round it, touching the shiny black paint in awe, before the pilot stopped him.

'Don't touch. Top secret, young man!' he shouted, shooing the boy away.

'So's this,' said Ollie, not to be outdone, juggling one of the professor's llama spit balls from hand to hand.

The ball fell to the ground.

'Oops. That wasn't supposed to happen.' Ollie looked up guiltily. But nobody seemed to notice the small puff of yellow smoke and he sidled back to the prime minister's speech.

★

'So I would like you all to join me,' said the PM, raising his glass, 'in a toast.'

Toast? thought Spud. *Where?*

'To the British government's finest secret agents. Agent GM451 and her puppies, Star and Spud.'

'Agent GM451, Star and Spud,' murmured the crowd.

And everyone drank and cheered.

'Erm, Mum.' Ollie tugged on Mrs Cook's best dress.

'Not now, Ollie,' she said, patting him on the head before turning to the prime minister. 'Would you like some cake, sir?'

'It's one of my best recipes,' Mrs Brown added. 'Double chocolate and marshmallow cake!'

Spud licked his chops hungrily.

'No, thank you,' said the prime minister, glancing at his watch. 'Must go. Things to do. Country to run.'

'You can have a bounce on my trampoline before you go, if you want, Your Highness,' offered Ollie.

'I'll pass,' smiled the prime minister as his aide ushered him out through the garden gate.

The helicopter blades whirred into action and the PM and his aides lowered their heads against the force of the draught as they walked across the field, not noticing the shiny pile of slippery goo that lay ahead, sparkling in the sun.

Ollie held his breath. One of the agents was first to go. His feet went from under him and he landed on his backside. The PM was next, tripping over the secret agent face first into the goo. It took nearly ten minutes for the small gang to stop slithering around and make it into the helicopter.

When Mr and Mrs Cook, faces bright red in

embarrassment, managed to stop apologizing, the sleek, black and orange helicopter eventually took off from the field behind the house and flew towards London.

The prime minister waved, but Ollie couldn't help noticing his teeth were clenched.

Mrs Brown decided to rescue the moment. She cut her chocolate cake into slices and gave the biggest one to Spud. 'That's to say sorry for thinking you had hurt Marmalade, when really you were saving him from that horrible bird.'

'Apology accepted,' woofed Spud, before burying his face in his cake. Marmalade came to sit beside him, daintily eating the bits that fell from the plate.

'I bet Harriet Hawk, Dumbbell and Squat won't be getting treats like this in prison,' said Sophie, licking chocolate from her fingers.

'I think I'm going to get that spare tyre back, dear,' said Mr Cook, going for a second slice of cake.

'That's all right,' said Mrs Cook. 'I prefer you cuddly.'

'What about you, Ma?' asked Star. 'Do you think you'll get your pooch paunch back?'

'Well, if I do,' woofed Lara, 'I won't be going to the gym to get rid of it. I've decided that gyms are very bad for my health!'